A Year in Our New Garden

Gerda Muller

A Year in Our New Garden

Gerda Muller

Floris Books

It was a big day for Anna and Benjamin – they were moving into their new house. Spring was coming and they couldn't wait to play in their garden.

"I love it here!" shouted Anna, as she leapt from the van.

"But the garden's a mess," grumbled Benjamin.

"Think how much fun we'll have making it beautiful!" said their mother, smiling.

A few days later, after everything was unpacked, they started to plan their new garden.

"I'd like a little plot all of my own," said Benjamin.

"Me too," said Anna. "Somewhere to grow vegetables!"

"I'd like lots of grass and flowers, and a patio," said their mother.

They drew it all on paper. It looked like this:

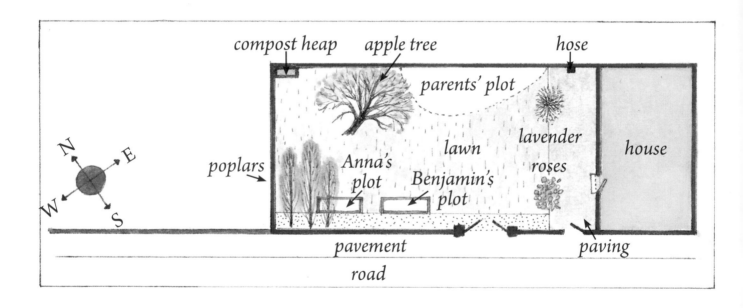

Anna and Benjamin drew their own plots too:

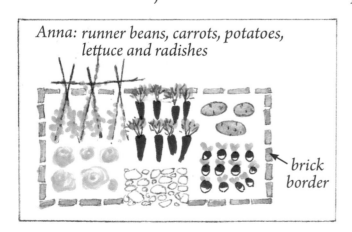

Anna: runner beans, carrots, potatoes, lettuce and radishes

brick border

Benjamin: lots of flowers, a little fir tree and a pond

When they woke the next morning, they couldn't wait to get started.

Anna and Benjamin began clearing away bits of junk. They found old tins, plastic bottles and even a mouldy sock – ew!

Their mother bought some garden tools.

Then they all set to work. Their father dug the soil with the spade, Anna sprinkled compost and Benjamin pulled up weeds.

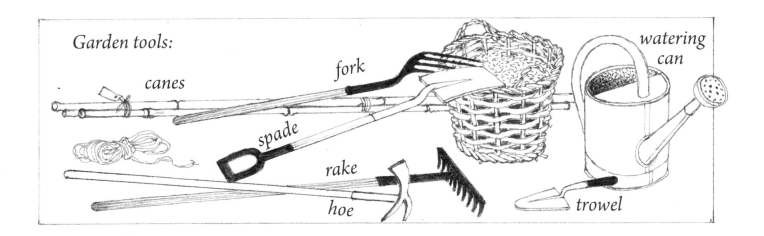

Garden tools: canes   fork   spade   rake   hoe   trowel   watering can

sowing grass seeds

raking them in

rolling the soil

watering

The patio was soon laid but it took a few weeks for the lawn to grow. Eventually it got so long it needed mowing.

scaring off birds

mowing

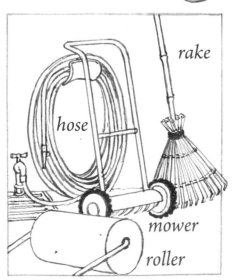

rake

hose

mower

roller

At last Anna and Benjamin had a lovely green carpet to lie on when the sun shone.

Their mother was worried about the old apple tree. "It's beautiful but it doesn't look very well," she said.

She called a gardener and he came to check the bark. The inside of the tree trunk was damp and teeming with ladybugs.

"Time for you to fly away now!" said Anna.

The gardener applied a paste to the trunk to protect it from the rain and help it heal. "Don't worry, your tree will get better soon!" he promised.

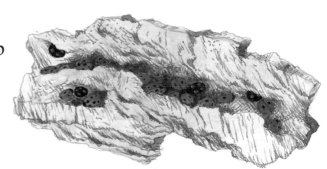

The apple tree was soon healthy again. It blossomed in the spring sunshine and the children invited their friends over to play in the garden.

Aunt Lisa also came to visit, and she brought some exciting gifts! Seedlings and a small fir tree for Benjamin, and some seed potatoes for Anna.

The children got straight to work, digging and planting.

The next day, Anna and Benjamin went to buy some seeds so they could grow more flowers and vegetables. But there were too many to choose from!

"For your sunny plot, Benjamin, I recommend marigolds, nasturtiums, cosmos and poppies," said the store manager.

"Could I try radishes, carrots, beans and chives?" asked Anna, thinking of her plan.

"Yes, that's a good mix," he replied.

The children couldn't wait to start planting. At home they tore the packets open.

"Look, Anna," said Benjamin. "Each type of seed is a different shape!"

Anna was busy trying to read the instructions. "It's too complicated!"

"I'll do it," said Benjamin impatiently, reaching over to grab the packet from her hand.

TWHACK!

They bumped into each other, scattering packets and seeds everywhere. Anna shouted and hurled herself at her brother, who pulled her hair and pushed her back.

"Hey! Stop fighting!" called a voice from high above their heads.

They looked up. A boy was waving from the balcony next door.

"Come on up, I'll give you some gardening tips," he called.

"Hi, I'm Louis," said their neighbour as soon as he opened his apartment door.

"I'm Anna and this is Benjamin," said Anna.

"You have so many plants on your balcony!" said Benjamin.

Cress sandwich: grow some cress on damp cotton wool (cotton) until it is 3 cm (1 inch) high. Cut, wash and sprinkle on top of buttered bread. Voilà!

"Gardening is my favourite thing. That's why I wanted to help you. Now, who wants a cress sandwich?" asked Louis, smiling.

Anna and Benjamin had never had cress before.

"It tastes like spring!" said Anna, and Benjamin patted his tummy in agreement.

They munched away while Louis showed them how to sow their seeds.

Aunt Lisa arrived later that day to find
Benjamin and Anna quietly raking and
watering their gardens.

"Look at you both hard at work!" she said.

Then they heard a shout from above. "Ding
dong! Special delivery!"

Louis was lowering a little basket on a rope.
Inside they found some tulips, cress seeds and
a book called *How Does My Garden Grow?*

"Wow!" shouted the children. "Thank you
very much, Louis!"

Summer came, and one beautiful morning the whole family were out gardening together.

"My radishes are ready!" Anna sang. "And they're big ones!"

"We could eat these dandelion weeds as well," said their mother. "We'll put them in a salad."

"Let's make enough for Louis too," said Anna. "I'll take it up afterwards."

After lunch, Anna found Louis on his balcony playing with his binoculars.

"Yum! That looks delicious!" he said as she handed him the radish and dandelion salad. "Here, take a look at your apple tree through these…"

"There are baby birds in the branches!" cried Anna.

The little birds hopped from twig to twig like acrobats, cheeping and chirping.

"Aren't they cute?" said Louis. "They're practising flying while they wait for their parents to bring them food."

"We could feed them! I'll bake some bread," said Anna.

"Actually, they prefer eating insects – which is good for your garden," laughed Louis.

"At night, do they sleep in their nest?" asked Anna.

"No, once they're old enough to leave the nest, they sleep outside and snuggle up together to keep warm."

In Benjamin's garden, the cosmos and poppies were already in bloom.
Bees buzzed and yellow butterflies floated around their colourful petals
all day long.

But there was always something more to do in the garden! Benjamin
planted new flowers from Louis, Anna tied her runner beans to their canes,
and their mother pulled out weeds.

That afternoon, Anna, Benjamin and Louis watched garden birds together. A couple of blackbirds were enjoying a picnic of worms, and pigeons were cooing on the grass nearby. Sparrows fluttered in the sand. There was also a greenfinch collecting some food.

"He'll get plump then fly south for the winter in a few weeks," said Louis. "They don't like the cold."

On the hottest day of the year, Benjamin and Anna invited friends over for a picnic. Louis was away on holiday with his family.

Anna made each of her guests a crown from leaves and flowers, and they ate a feast of cherries and homemade lemonade.

Benjamin buried a cherry stone in the soil beside him. "Let's see if this grows into a cherry tree so we can eat our own cherries one day," he said.

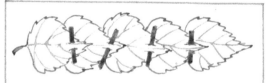

How to make Anna's crown: find some big leaves and flowers and place them in a line. Pin with matchsticks.

How to make Benjamin's lemonade: squeeze lemons, add fizzy water and cubes of fruit, then sweeten with a sprinkle of sugar.

People get hot and thirsty in the summer, and so does the garden. The children had to water it every day. Luckily, there were plenty of fun ways to do the job – and cool down at the same time. No one could escape Louis' rainstorms!

One warm evening, while moths were fluttering around the candle, Benjamin and Anna's father said he had something to show them.

He placed a heavy object in each child's hand. "Look what I found underneath the old apple tree…"

"It's treasure!" cried Benjamin.

"Maybe," said their father. "These coins are more than a hundred years old!"

Before he went to bed, Benjamin held his coin tightly in his hand and looked out at the old tree.

"Imagine all the things it has seen," he murmured to himself.

Three types of moth:

the brown-neck

the housekeeper (they like to come into your home!)

the alfafa looper moth

That night, Benjamin dreamt that he woke up beneath the old apple tree, and it began speaking to him.

"A lot has changed over the last hundred and twenty years," said the tree. "When I was planted, the town was much smaller and quieter. Back then people travelled by horse and cart. Children hung lanterns in my branches and played around me."

The branches swayed in the breeze and Benjamin thought he saw little lanterns twinkling like stars.

"Then, for a long time, I was alone," said the tree. "Nobody climbed my branches or picked my apples. I was ill, and thought I wouldn't make it through another winter. Until your family came! Now you've brought laughter back into the garden, and helped me get better too!"

In the morning, Benjamin woke up in his bed, as usual, smiling.

Dear Ben[jamin]
Over the last few days, two types of flowers have scattered their seeds. The wind spread them far and wide!

Hope you're having fun, Louis

Guess what I saw today! A butterfly landing on a flower and drinking nectar with its long tongue. It looked like this:

See you soon, Louis

Later that summer, the whole family went on holiday to the seaside. They asked Louis to watch over the garden from his balcony and, while they were away, he wrote them letters:

Dear Benjamin and Anna,
Today I went to the park and found some strange mushrooms called 'Shaggy Ink Caps'. They're called that because a kind of ink flows from their tops.
Then I looked at birch seeds with a magnifying glass: they're shaped like butterflies and they fly like them too!
Bye! Louis

Dear Benjamin and Anna,
The primroses are in flower. I'm going to try and make models of them!
I also found lots of ladybugs. They're usually black, orange or red, with two to seven spots, and they like to eat aphids all day long.
See you soon, Louis

Hello!
Guess what I found in a hole in the wall... A little fern! And what does [it] have unde[r] each leaf? Tiny spores!
One other thing, I've found o[ut] that tomatoes, potatoes and beans come all the way from South America! I've drawn you a picture of us as three Native Americans cooking by the fire.

Benjamin   Anna   Lou[is]

Soon, Anna and Benjamin were back at home. They had collected a sea urchin, a starfish and some seaweed for Louis, to say thank you for his letters.

It had been so hot that Anna's vegetables had shrivelled, Benjamin's flowers had wilted and the fir tree had died.

"Don't worry," said their father. "Summer plants dying is a natural part of the changing seasons."

"Look at this!" called Anna. "My potatoes are fine!"

Sure enough, the potatoes had survived deep underground where it had stayed cooler.

Autumn arrived, and Benjamin and Anna invited some friends round to build a campfire.

"Remember," said their father, "you must always have a bucket of water near the fire, just in case."

They roasted chestnuts and ate them with mulberries, hazelnuts and apple tart – filled with apples from their very own tree!

Then they used autumn nuts to make necklaces, little boats and dangling spiders!

At the end of the day, Benjamin poured his bucket of water over the fire to put it out.

A necklace made from acorn shells and beans.

A spider made from a horse chestnut and pins.

A boat made from a walnut shell, a matchstick and paper for the sail.

A few days later, their father was busy building a box in the corner of the garden.

"What's that for?" asked Benjamin.

"We're going to fill it with dead leaves and flowers, and they will slowly turn into compost that will help new plants grow," he said.

"We're making plant food!" said Benjamin, and he began sweeping up all the dead leaves in the garden.

Their father had also made a bird table so Anna and Benjamin could feed nuts and seeds to the birds through winter.

"Dinner's ready, little birds!" Anna called.

For Louis' ninth birthday, Benjamin and Anna sent a basket up to him. Inside was a sunflower head and a drawing.

"Thank you!" called Louis. "Now the birds can feast on sunflower seeds up here too!"

There was still so much to do before winter: Benjamin pulled up all the dead flowers in his garden, and then buried hyacinth, tulip and daffodil bulbs deep underground, where it is warmer in winter.

"These flowers will send up shoots to let us know when spring has arrived!"

Their mother hung all her everlastings upside down to make dried flower bouquets. Benjamin added some heather and lavender, closed his eyes and breathed deeply.

"Do you know why I love autumn?" he asked. "Because it smells so good!"

One windy day, Aunt Lisa took Benjamin and Anna for a walk in the countryside. They made bows and arrows from fallen branches and hid among the trees.

"We're trapping bears!" shouted Benjamin.

"And hunting boars!" cried Anna.

"Come on, children!" called Aunt Lisa. "It looks like it's going to rain."

When the rain started, it didn't stop for days.

Mushrooms sprung up in the soggy lawn. The wind howled and damp leaves littered the garden.

Anna spotted something else… a little greenfinch had died among the flowers.

"It must've been injured," said her father when she brought it to him. "It didn't fly away with the others."

"We should bury it at the end of the garden," said Anna.

While their father dug a hole for the bird, Benjamin read a poem he had written specially:

This wet and windy autumn day,
A little bird has passed away.
When leaves take on a golden hue,
Oh little bird, we'll think of you.

Two weeks before Christmas, Benjamin woke up early to an exciting surprise.

"Anna, look outside!"

The garden was covered in a beautiful blanket of bright white snow. It was untouched – apart from hundreds of tiny footprints!

"I think those smaller ones belong to the blackbirds," said Anna.

"And the big ones must be pigeons," said Benjamin.

That afternoon their friends came to play. They threw snowballs and even built a snow-bear!

Benjamin and Anna knew they would have a wonderful winter in their garden.

When the winter snow melted, Benjamin's tulip, hyacinth and daffodil bulbs poked through the earth just as he had planned.

tulip   hyacinth   daffodil

Anna and Benjamin raced into the garden to see them.

"What shall we grow this year?" asked Benjamin.

At that moment, Aunt Lisa arrived with a basketful of flower seedlings ready for planting.

"Perfect timing, Aunt Lisa," said Anna. "Let's get started!"

The
End

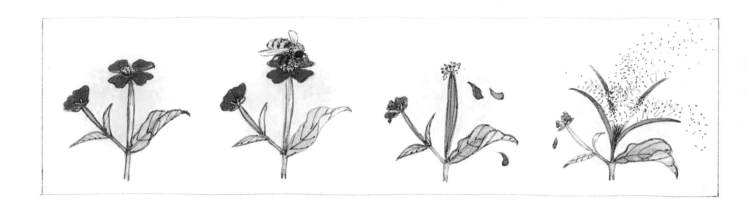

Pollen

When flowers open, insects fly into them to drink their nectar. Pollen sticks to their hairy bodies and legs.

That pollen rubs off onto other flowers the insect visits. This fertilises the flowers, which turn into fruit containing seeds.

When fruit is ripe, it springs open or rots to free the seeds. The wind, animals and birds scatter the seeds on the soil, like gardeners do!

If the soil is fertile, the seeds will grow into new plants. Soil is fertile when it is full of the minerals and nutrients plants need to grow well.

Sowing seeds

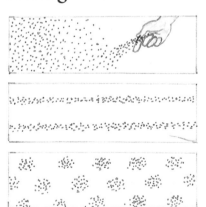

For grass, scatter seeds evenly.

For carrots, dig straight furrows and scatter the seeds in lines.

For runner beans, place seeds in little holes at regular intervals.

Cover the seeds with earth and water well.

Roots

A plant must have strong roots to hold it firmly in place and take in nutrients. But roots aren't all the same: tulip roots come from a round bulb in the ground but ivy roots cling to walls.

Louis' balcony

Spring flowers

Daffodils, tulips, honeysuckle, forget-me-nots, hyacinths, pansies, cress and primroses.

Summer flowers

Everlastings, honeysuckle, sweet peas, sunflowers, nasturtiums, fringed pinks, geraniums, petunias, marigolds.

Herbs

Thyme   Parsley   Mint   Chives

For Marianne and Hélène

First published in 1988 in German as
Ein Garten für Kinder in der Stadt
First published in English by Floris Books in 2016
© 1988, 2016 Gerda Muller
Gerda Muller has asserted her right under the Copyright, Designs and Patents Act
1988 to be recognised as the Author and Illustrator of this Work
www.florisbooks.co.uk
British Library CIP Data available
ISBN 978-178250-259-3
Printed in Poland